SATAN'S TORMENT

THE RAINE MICHELSON FILES

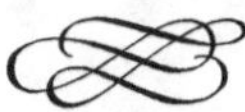

DYLAN KEEFER

Demon's Match

Satan's Torment

Devil's Advocate

Lucifer's Wake

Mischief Miles Investigations

A Familiar Scent

Breaking and Entering

Like Father, Like Son

Too Close For Comfort

Mr. Right or Mr. Wrong

Everscape Online

Traitor of Golden Blaze

Queen of Ragnarok

Champion of Everscape

Britney Allen: The London Crime Syndicate

Blood of Babes: The Slasher Files

Standalone

Lost in Space

The Lone Survivor

Mr. Buddy Bot

Evelyn

I dedicate this book to my friends and family who have always supported in my dream of being a professional author.

— DYLAN KEEFER

SATAN'S TORMENT

DYLAN KEEFER

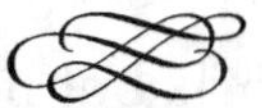

Open your eyes.

That was what her brain was telling her to do. At least, that's what the voice in her head seemed to be saying. She wasn't quite sure. Everything was in a fog. Everything felt heavy. Then she realized why her eyelids didn't want to pop open. A headache. It was a subtle throb that didn't make itself known until it was beating at the sides of her skull like a jackhammer trying to break ground. No light appeared from behind the curtain of her eyelids. That either meant it was night or there were no windows in whatever dark hole she was in.

Dammit, Heather, open your eyes!

She obeyed. Her body voluntarily jerked as consciousness became her friend again. Groaning, the girl tried to control the fear that immediately gripped her inside. She couldn't feel her arms or hands. The rope that bound them together behind her back was unforgiving. If it weren't for the numbness, it would probably hurt a lot. Her feet and legs were bound in the same manner causing her to sit up in an abnormally straight position with her head the only thing free to move.

Shit! The room was dark, but her eyes quickly adjusted. She was in some sort of basement. His basement? There hadn't been much of a glimpse—well, not a sober one.

"Hey! Hello!" Her voice seemed to hit a wall. No echo. No other sound. Was she in a soundproof room? "Is anyone there? Please!"

She tried to focus on moving her fingers. Maybe she could reach the ropes and somehow free herself. Her hands were too numb. She relaxed. There was no use fighting it right now. She needed to think. Dumb headache. She listened in silence for a while with her head leaned back. How long had it been since the party? There had been a lot of drinking which she had planned to avoid, but that hadn't gone the way she wanted.

"Heather, you need to chill out. You know that Eddie just needs to blow off some steam." She sat pouting in Tisha's car with her arms crossed.

"That's not the point," Heather muttered. "The point is that he expects way too much out of this relationship. Unrealistic things."

"You are marrying him, aren't you?" Heather nodded slowly. They were engaged and had been for over a year.

She had pushed for them to get married for them to get married right away, but he had wanted to wait. He had training to go through, then he was looking at deployment, and then things just kept coming up. She had warned him that the longer he waited, the harder this relationship was going to be—not for him, but for her. "You guys are high school sweethearts. The 'it' couple. I think you can make it through a fight about..."

"I cheated on him," Heather blurted out. Tisha turned quickly in her seat with mouth wide open.

"You what? Heather!"

"Don't act surprised," Heather sighed. "Everyone thought I was doing it in high school and college. Why not now?"

"But I knew you weren't," her friend said. "When?"

"You don't want to know," Heather said, but Tisha gave her a look that said she wasn't dropping the subject. Heather dropped her head. "Remember that dinner thing we had at Celina and Dave's? Everybody was there?"

"Oh no," Tisha groaned. "You hooked up with that guy Joe, didn't you?"

Heather shook her head and bit her lip. "Worse. I— hooked up with Dave."

Tisha sat back in the driver's seat and ran her hands through her hair. "Heather. What. The. Hell."

"I know," Heather groaned.

"He's not only married, but you and I were Celina's freaking bridesmaids!"

"I know. I know."

"You know, but..." Tisha closed her mouth and breathed several times through her nose. "So, Eddie has a right to be upset that you are a little too free with other guys. He's been faithful to you, and you've been a whore."

They sat in silence for a moment. Parked on the side of a main street in front of a bar that held a bunch of their friends celebrating a going away party. They were all dressed up, but now the mood had changed. "It was a mistake, Tisha. You know that I love Eddie, but I messed up. I know that." "And what are you going to do about it?" Her friend didn't look at her but merely stared ahead at the traffic. "I'm going to tell him." "Tonight?" Heather nodded to her friend. "But can we just go in and make tonight about our friend leaving. That's it." In answer, Tisha grabbed the door handle and got out of the car. Heather jerked again. This time, it was the sound of a door opening. Light poured into the basement illuminating just how dark and dusty it really was. She squinted as a shadow filled the doorway and took each step slowly. "Who are you? Why are you doing this?" Her voice quivered as his steps grew closer. His features weren't clearly seen until he stood directly in front of her and reached over her head. There was a small snap, and a light came on from the pull of a string she had not noticed. Heather shivered. He was really handsome—strong, chiseled features, fit but not too muscular, deep eyes. And she knew what had happened.

"Hello, Heather," he said walking over to pull up a chair

that was behind her. "How are you feeling? You were asleep for a while." "Why are you doing this to me?" He dragged the chair around her and placed it in front so that when he sat, his knees almost touched her own. "Do you remember me? Do you remember what happened at all?" She swallowed hard as he smiled. "I guess, you might still be a little foggy. I'm the guy at the party tonight that you were flirting with quite heavily." "I wasn't flir--"He smacked her on the cheek. It wasn't hard, but it was enough to get her attention. "You were, Heather. Blame it on the drinks you had, but the truth is that you are a natural flirt and whore. That's why your fiance didn't go with you to the party, and Tisha did."

"How—How do you know all of this? I don't understand."

"Of course, you don't. You're all alike, aren't you? And I guess I'm the one that has to make an example of you. Just like I have to do with her."

Heather jumped slightly as he reached around and wrenched her hand. He pulled off the engagement ring and held it to her face.

"This isn't a symbol of love to you. It's a symbol of you convincing another man that you will be true to him when you won't!" He was getting louder, and she didn't know what he was going to do next. "But I'm going to convince him this time. Eddie is going to come to his senses and realize that you aren't worthy of love. And when I do, then you'll get what you deserve."

He turned the ring in between his fingers, almost mesmerized by its beauty. Heather gulped and sniffed back the sobs that were trying to find their way out. "Please, I don't know what you want me to do, but I'll do it. I'll do it just please, let me go." He closed his hand around the ring and looked at the pleading girl. She shook her head and whispered her, please. They feel on deaf ears. He stood up and kicked the chair away. "Too late."

Sleep seemed to come a little bit easier tonight. That didn't mean, he slept. Eli had gotten used to the fact that he never really slept throughout the night. The only time he came remotely close to that bliss was when a plan came together, and at that particular moment, his plan sat in his basement. He had untied her with the promise that if she caused any trouble, she would regret it. The girl had been very compliant. She knew. She knew that she was the reason she was in this spot. Though he may seem like a monster, he was helping people. That's all he wanted to do.

Eli turned his head. It was five forty-nine. The sun would be up sooner or later, but his first errand of the day wouldn't be open yet. Maybe a good run and a shower would help. Maybe, she would be ready for some breakfast.

"Hey, Mike. Haven't seen you run in a while." Jess Winchester and her husband, Todd waved at Eli as he stretched in his driveway. He smiled and waved back.

"I know. I've slacked off a little bit but found some motivation today. How are you guys doing?"

"Great," Todd said as they stood by their car. "We're taking the kids to Arizona to see some family tomorrow through next week. Both of us finally got off work and decided a little family vacation would be nice."

"Maybe a date night or two if we leave the kids with their cousins," Jess said with a twinkle in her eye. Eli smiled.

"It's awesome that you both still do date nights. You both are a model couple," he said. "I hope you guys enjoy your trip. Tell the kids hey for me."

Their car sped past him while he set a pace for his six-mile run. It had taken some time for him to establish himself in this neighborhood. A change in appearance, style, mannerisms, and everything that Eli Samuels stood for and could be known for was erased. To the Winchesters and other neighbors, he was a widower who moved to Hawaii from Louisiana and owned his own marketing business. He worked mainly from home and did a lot of traveling. No one knew who he was—who he really was. No one.

If Marjorie Samuels were still alive, she would have done everything in her power to stop him from what he was doing. She had been a devout Catholic ever since she was a schoolgirl and had tried to get her son and daughter to follow God and the church ever since they were young. Bill Samuels, wasn't religious about anything but his wife. So, even though he didn't believe in God or the church, he went for Marjorie's peace of mind. And everything had been picture perfect—until young Eli's perfect picture had been shattered.

Six miles wasn't a challenge, but the morning was in full swing, and he needed to get going with his plan. After a warm shower, Eli started breakfast. It had already been several months without Becca, and in that time, he had become a decent cook. Though he hadn't planned on being alone so soon, he knew that ultimately, he had to finish this alone. No woman would understand. There was some unwritten law where all women stood together no matter what. He hated the feminist who claimed that they were oppressed. The blacks and the Jews could claim it, and even the gays could claim it in some fashion over the women. But women, especially white women, were not oppressed. He was all for the downfall of chauvinistic bureaucracy, but that was not the majority.

He scraped the last of the eggs onto a second plate before balancing both plates on one arm and holding his handgun in the other. Heather scampered to the far side of the basement when he walked down the stairs. Eli waved the gun at her.

"Come on. You gotta eat." He placed the pate on the floor and then sat down Indian-style in front of it. He took his fork and started to stab at the food on his plate. He chomped on it greedily before looking back up at her. She hadn't moved. "I'm going to be gone all day, so you need to eat. I'm not reheating it for you." "Please," was all she could say. He kept eating. Eventually, she would learn that he did not pity her. He did not feel sorry for her. She was in the wrong, and he was trying to do the right thing.

The smell of the food was too enticing, and the girl slowly walked up and got on her knees in front of the plate. She peered at him through messy strands of hair and saw him nod to the plate. Heather took a hold of it, and once one fork-full of the food hit her mouth, she started to wolf-down the rest.

"I'm not sure how long I'm going to keep you down here," Eli spoke as if this were an amicable conversation. "Eddie has his weekly basketball night with the guys, right? I think I'll start after that. I wanna leave him with clues about your past and present. I don't think I should start off with your thing with Dave. I should wait, and maybe reveal that to him somehow tomorrow. I'll just make sure he gets some shots of those pics you used to send that one guy in college while you were dating." Heather lowered her plate. Her face grew pale. "Why would you—how could you..."

Eli shrugged. "Really, Heather, it's more like 'how could you?'. If we are pointing fingers here, I mean."

"You're going to ruin a relationship because—what— you're too sick in the head to have one of your own?"

Eli ate his last bit of sausage and shook his head. "No.

See, you ruined this Heather. You did." He reached for her plate quickly which hadn't been finished. "And for that comment, you don't get any more until I get home."

She remained on her knees as he left the room and locked the door behind him. Maybe she wasn't going to learn. Somehow, she seemed to still think that he was the bad guy. It would take a day or two. He had time.

Eli pulled out his phone and sat down at the kitchen table after the dishes were put away. He hummed Aerosmith to himself as he waited for the phone to ring. On the third one, she picked up.

"Hello, this is Hanna." Eli closed his eyes and focused on her voice. It sounded so beautiful. For the longest time, he would dream of just seeing her and being in her embrace again. He remembered every single moment.

"Elijah, is this you?" His eyes opened. He heard her sigh. "Elijah, please talk to me. I know you're the one that's been calling every week. I don't know how I know, but I do. Eli, I know what they're saying about you on the news. I don't believe it. I know you. I do, but I—also know that you've disappeared. You can tell me what's going on. I can help you. Please!"

He hung up the phone. For a moment, he sat there and just thought about the sound of her voice. It always comforted him. It always soothed him. The one woman that was always faithful. He scrolled through the phone and dialed another number. This one only rang once before being picked up.

"Raine Michelson speaking."

"Hello, Dr. Michelson. You sound chipper today." There was a pause over the phone, and Eli smiled. "I hope I'm not interrupting something. I just wanted to say that tonight I'll have a surprise for you. I hope you don't mind staying up a little bit past..."

"I'm not playing your games anymore," Raine growled into the phone. "You are going to get what's coming for you."

"I think that you're going to get what's coming for you, actually," Eli said. "Honestly, I do know that the last few have been bad, but you still haven't learned your lesson."

"I confessed everything," Raine said with exasperation. "I have no other secrets to reveal. You won."

"Confessing is not the same as learning. You've changed nothing. You've righted no wrong. You've suffered nothing."

"What do you want from me!" He let her frustration ring in his ears. What did he want? He wanted everything to go back to what it was supposed to be like. He wanted the life he should have had. He wanted his mother.

"You aren't ready," he said hearing her groan. "When you are, you'll know. Until then..."

He hung up the phone. Time to go.

* * *

"So, what's her name?"

Micah looked around at the several pairs of eyes staring at him over the table on the back porch. He picked up his beer.

"What are you talking about?" As soon as he put the bottle to his lips, Kyle laughed.

"I told you that he would take a drink when I asked him! That's his tell!" The others at the table laughed. Micah frowned.

"What? I don't have a tell." "You have a tell," Rachel laughed. "Why do you think you always lose at card games with the family? It starts off as a tell; then you are just too buzzed to play well."

"She's got you there," Kyle nodded. "Before it was beer, it was milk. Dammit, if we didn't have to but an extra half gallon of milk just for you."

"Listen, I didn't fly all the way here from Hawaii just to be ganged up on. Pete, help me out here."

Pete sat back in his chair with a smile. "No, I'm curious, too. Who is she? Who is the girl that has you nervous to talk about her?"

For the record, this was why Micah kept his personal life secret—or at least tried to. He knew that once these three knew, the whole family would know. Soon, his mother would be posting a picture and update in the next family newsletter.

"Fine," he mumbled. "Her name is Raine."

"Raine, that's pretty," Rachel said. "How did you meet?"

"We met on a case."

"So, she works with you?" Kyle said. Micah shook his head.

"No. I mean, kinda. There's a complicated thing going on here." It was apparent that Micah wasn't going to escape the evening without telling them what was going on, so, he gave in and told them about everything that had happened.

"You weren't lying about complicated," Pete said. Micah nodded to his cousin.

"It's not complicated," Kyle snorted. They all looked at him. "What? Micah, you are in love with this girl. Somehow, this guy—this Eli Samuels—is winning. You said that he says he is doing this because these girls aren't worthy of the love these faithful guys give. Right now, he's convinced her that he's right. You've got to convince her that he's not."

Rachel got out of her seat and kissed Kyle on the lips. "My genius husband."

"Genius? No. All this time reading books on psych and philosophy have just gotten to my head. My students never have any idea of what the hell they walk into each semester."

It was truly amazing what Kyle had made of himself after the accident that ended his dreams of becoming a cop. Micah was sure that he couldn't do it. Kyle had studied psychology and philosophy, become a professor, and married a wonderful girl who adored him and was faithful to him even in his condition.

"So, do I need to come down to Hawaii and help you

catch this guy—and catch this girl?" Kyle joked as Pete and Rachel cleaned dishes in the kitchen. Micah snorted a laugh.

"I think I've got it," he said. Kyle nodded.

"Yeah, you do. Just go with your heart on it. Win her back from wherever she is trapped from."

That whole conversation had been playing in a loop in Micah's mind since he had been back in Hawaii. Things had been very casual lately between the two of them. That partly had to do with their jobs, and partly had to do with what Kyle had so aptly deduced when he had been up there. She was keeping the search for Eli away from him, and though he wanted to help, he understood why she was dangling it at arm's length.

"Next in line." He sighed. The bank was unusually busy for a Tuesday morning. He thought that getting an early start might be the smart thing, and it looked like it wasn't an original thought. Pulling out his phone, he texted Tai that he would be late getting into work. Sliding the device back in his pocket, Micah glanced around the building. His eyes fixed on the man a few people ahead of him. Something about him seemed unnatural. His appearance seemed normal, but the way he carried himself didn't seem like it fit him. Sheesh. He had been spending too much time around Raine. She would look at this guy and try to analyze why he might feel awkward in his own skin. He looked like he worked out, but was it for pleasure or duty? He wore glasses.

Could he not wear contacts or did he think the glasses were more stylish?

"Next." Micah stepped forward, but his attention shifted again to the door as three individuals walked in one right after the other. If slow motion were actually a valid option, he would have noted everything before it happened. The security guard pulling out his gun. The identical, dark clothing and masks. The look on the one man's eyes that showed desperation and determination. But it happened a lot faster, and before he could react, the first gunshot had dropped the security guard, and the crowd in the bank dropped with startled screams. He started to reach for his own weapon but stopped. It was too dangerous to escalate this even further with innocent civilians around. Better to play nice for now. He got down on the floor, too. "Everybody against the far wall near those offices! Anyone in offices, get out here now!" One of the robbers. "Tellers! You, too!"

Micah moved with the rest of them and kept his head low. Sliding down into a seated position, he noticed that he was right beside the man he was looking at earlier. The two of them locked eyes, and Micah felt his heart beat go even faster than it was already going. As if this situation couldn't get any worse. He would have never recognized him if he hadn't been close enough to look into his eyes.

" Lieutenant Micah Duscane," the man whispered with a slight annoyance. Micah mimicked it.

"Eli Samuels."

CHAPTER TWO

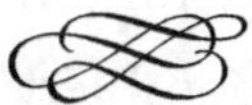

ai dropped the deceptively heavy bag into the trunk of the car and slammed it with authority. A layer of sweat came off of his face with one swipe, and he muttered something under his breath.

"What was that Tai," Raine smiled with a gleam in her eye. "I said no one needs dat much stuff fo one trip," he waved her off. "Malanie act like she gonna go away fo eva."

Raine slapped him on the back and then cringed as she removed a sweaty hand and wiped it off on a dry spot on his shirt. "Hate to break it to you big guy, but this is just for one summer. Wait until she leaves for college."

Tai shook his head. "Malanie gonna go to da Unaversidy uh Hawaii. She'll be right here."

Raine gave a slight nod but turned quickly to the teenager rushing out of the front door of the Ulafala's house. She stood by as Tai gave the girl some last minute instructions and then gave her a hug before walking away.

"Super sentimental, Tai," Raine called out as the big man flipped her off on his way to the front door.

"You know Tai," Malanie laughed. "He doesn't like emotion that he can't make fun of."

"You're telling me? When I left Hawaii to go home after the case with you, he wouldn't say a nice word to me the whole time after I told him I was going. He takes it rough."

Malanie sighed. "Rough. He still thinks I'm going to attend the University of Hawaii after I graduate."

Raine laughed. The pride she had for Malanie couldn't be described. The Ulafala's may have adopted her, but Raine claimed her as her own. After she had testified against her mother, Malanie had grown closer to Raine. She had become a study partner, gossip girl, confident, and big sister; and it has been a struggle for Raine to balance their time together. She needed to make sure that Malanie had friends her own age and didn't just connect with her. Her undefined relationship with Micah wasn't going to work, and as much as she loved Tai, she couldn't be besties with him and stay sane.

"You wanna go get drinks?"

The question had come right out of the blue. Raine dropped the towel from her face and looked into the deep brown eyes of the woman standing in front of her.

"You're talking to me?"

"Yeah," the woman laughed as she popped her hip out and took a drink of water.

"Drinks?"

"I've been watching you since you joined this spin class, and well, you're different than everyone else here. You aren't here for exercise. I know, because no one else zones out the entire class and only checks back in when it's over. We're all struggling to survive, and you make it look easy."

Raine smirked and crossed her arms. *Okay, smart stuff, let's see how observant you are.* "And just what have you concluded about me since you have been watching me the entire time?"

"Oh, you make me sound like a stalker," the woman laughed.

"Okay, well, I believe that you work at a very stressful job, you don't have a lot of friends, the friends you do have are probably centered around a complicated relationship. Going out on a limb, but I also believe that you live alone in an apartment with a fish."

"A fish," Raine frowned. "Why a fish?"

"If you had a dog or cat, you'd be with them right now instead of at a spin class after work. You don't want something that you have to really take time to care for because you are pre-occupied with something else."

The fish thing was on point. Raine had bought one a little over three weeks ago. However, Skittles had died two days ago, and she felt that she had failed him. Of course, when Tai had heard, he made some joke about how Skittles was now really tasting the rainbow.

"I'm was a theater and dance major in college, and currently not doing anything related to either. So, I have no room to judge; only to drink."

That had been the start of Raine finding a friend. Malanie looked at her now with some concern.

"You're not going to get all emotional on me, are you? I'm just going to teach swimming at a camp; not going off to war."

"Yeah, well," Raine sighed. "Just remember that if anything happens to you, Tai is going to be a mess, and no one has time for that."

The two embraced, and Raine watched as Malanie pulled off. As the car was disappearing in the distance, her phone rang in the pocket of her shorts. She reached to get it and caught it on the last ring.

"Ailani? What's going on?"

"Raine, I need you downtown. We've got a bank robbery with hostages?"

"You! Get up!"

Shaky legs started to straighten as she used the wall to stand. Her hand whitened as she exerted pressure against the wall due to the fear of what the man pointing the gun at her was going to say next.

"Leave her alone," the woman next to her started to rise. "She's just a girl. She's..."

The gun pointed to the woman, and the gunman took a few steps towards them. "I didn't ask you to talk! Shut up and sit back down!"

"Mom, it's okay," the girl said. She pushed herself away from the wall and stepped over Micah's feet. He tensed up. She was just a kid. He desperately wanted to reach for the gun that was between his hip and the wall. The girl stood in front of the gunman trembling. His eyes peered at her through black stocking face mask. He held out a bag gripped in his free hand.

"Go around and gather anything electronic that any of these people have. Anything." She started to take the bag, but he didn't loosen his grip. "You miss anyone, and I will shoot them."

She nodded vigorously, and he released his grip on the bag. She quickly began to walk around the group of people huddled along the wall of the bank. Micah counted about twenty-six people including bank workers, and not including the dead security guard. There were three more robbers. All of them were armed.

"They haven't made any attempts to get money." Micah turned swiftly to see Eli Samuels adjusting his position with his back against the wall. His anger grew tenfold.

"What is this, Eli?" He growled. "What are you planning?"

Eli snorted. "You think I'm involved in a bank robbery? You act like I'm a criminal."

"You are a criminal. You've abducted, tortured, poisoned, and murdered people. Robbery isn't beneath you."

"As I just pointed out," Eli sighed. "This isn't a robbery. They haven't asked to see the vault, haven't asked for the tellers to empty bank bags, and they didn't question whether a silent alarm was hit."

Micah had to admit that he was right. Two of the bigger ones had carried the security guards body into one of the personal banker offices while the third stood peering out of the front of the bank.

"Don't just stand there," said the fourth who had initiated the young girl to grab their electronics. The third glanced back. "Pull down the shades along the windows. Make sure the cops won't be able to see inside. Check to make sure there are no surprise entrances."

The third set his gun down awkwardly on a chair and did what he was told. Micah looked up at the girl who now stood in front of him. She held open the bag; pleading with her eyes for him not to do anything that would cause the gunman to be angry with her.

"Don't worry, little girl," Eli whispered softly next to him. "This man is a cop."

Micah drove his elbow back, but Eli moved enough to where his elbow hit the wall causing a sharp stab of pain to erupt in that area. The girl's eyes grew wide as she glanced down at Micah's hip. She saw the gun.

"Hey! What's going on over there!" The girl turned and gripped his bag tightly.

"The man hit his elbow on the wall reaching for his cell phone." There was a normal tremble in her voice as Micah quickly reached for his phone and dropped it in the bag. Eli did the same thing. The gunman stared at them, and Micah felt the girl shift her foot next to his leg blocking any line sight to the gun.

"Hurry up, girl," the man growled. She nodded quickly and continued on.

"What the hell were you thinking?" Micah hissed.

Eli smirked. "I just wondered how you would react now knowing that this girl knows you are supposed to be the one to protect everyone. She is counting on you to be able to save her in this situation. You're now supposed to be the hero of this story. What happens if you aren't?"

* * *

THE SCENE in front of the bank was organized chaos. Traffic had been a nightmare to get through, and Raine hung on tight as Tai pushed his massive truck through any hole that even looked like it would accommodate him. The streets surrounding the bank were blocked off, and they made it as far as they could in the vehicle before making the last few hundred yards on foot.

Ailani was directing officers on what to do, and she could see the stress of protocol pouring out in frustration.

"You two finally got here." He pointed to Tai. "You took his truck, didn't you? That thing is not what you take when you want to get into downtown fast."

"Hey, brudda," Tai said with his head up. "My truck can do anything your little cop cars can."

"What's the situation, Ailani," Raine turned their attention back to the robbery.

"We don't know," Ailani said. "Windows are blocked. There is no way to tell how many hostages are in there; or robbers. It's quiet. A few pedestrians walking back said they heard a gunshot, and the silent alarm was pushed a minute after that."

"You call inside yet?"

Ailani nodded to her. "You're the best person for that, Raine. We've got all possible exits covered. We've got officers running license plates of all the cars in the lot."

Raine nodded. Ailani handed her a phone, and she sighed. Looking at the building, she gathered her wits about her before hitting the 'send' button. Her feet voluntarily tapped the concrete as she listened to the ringing. *C'mon. Pick up.* She almost hung up herself before she heard a click on the other end.

"Hello!" She said placing the phone up to her ear. "Hello, are you there?"

"Who is this?"The gruff voice sounded raspy. It wasn't a

smoker's rasp. The man's voice was wither going, or he was somewhat older in age.

"I'm outside of the bank right now," Raine said. "My name is Dr. Raine Michelson. What's your name?"

"That's not important right now." There was a deep breath over the phone. *This guy isn't a robber; at least not one who has done this before.*

"There are a lot of people in there that are probably scared," Raine said. "You wanna tell me what I can help you with so we can get them and you out of there safely?"

"You're not in control of this situation, darlin'. You need to listen to me. You understand?"

"I do," Raine said. She looked at the bank. None of the blinds had moved. He wasn't worried about the cops outside.

"I need three vials of a serum delivered to me within the next sixty minutes." Raine frowned. She wasn't expecting that. Ailani and Tai were staring at her with anxious looks. She turned her back to them as the man continued. "I know that it's being stored under guard at Tripler Army Medical Center by order of a Commander Walt Painter. It's called R33PM."

"A serum? That's what you want? That's all you want?" Raine shook her head. "Why take a bank filled with hostages for something like that?"

"You asked what I wanted, and that's what I want." The phone line disconnected, and Raine handed it back to Ailani.

"All of this is for a serum?" Ailani asked. Raine nodded. So this wasn't a robbery. It was the best way to get the police here quickly and where they could get easy hostages.

"Yeah," she said. "The guy sounds like he is from the mainland; which means that they traveled to get here. He said this thing is called R33PM, and it's being held at Tripler. He wants three vials in an hour."

"So, if they aren't dangerous, then we can make a move," a nearby officer spoke up. Ailani shot him a look.

"No, that is the worst thing. The problem with people who jumped into something like this is that they are unpredictable," he turned to Raine. "I'm going to get them looking at any rentals in the area."

"Probably should look into any taxi, uber, or lyft drop-offs around the area within a five minute time period." Raine looked at Tai. "Wanna help me find out what R33PM is?"

"I got you," Tai placed his fist on his chest. Ailani stepped away from them as Raine and Tai started to find an area away from the noise.

Raine glanced at the bank, and one of the cars parked close to it caught her eye. Micah and Tai argued about their cars enough that the Charger Micah drove was easy to spot from anywhere. Silver. Sunroof. Black car seats and steering wheel cover. Minnesota Vikings bumper sticker.

"Tai," Raine said quickly pulling out her cell phone. She heard the phone ringing but knew just by seeing the plates.

"Wat?" Tai stopped. He followed her finger as she

pointed to the Dodge sitting in front of the bank.

"Micah is in there."

* * *

So, Eli was right. The phone was slammed back on the receiver as robber number one joined his partners. Micah watches intently as the four of them came together and tried his best to make out the words being spoken softly.

"Are we good? Are they gonna get it?" said number four who now had the bag of cell phones from the girl.

"I dunno," number one said scratching his head. "I feel like they need to know that we're serious about all of this before they act. We might need to send a message."

"We aren't going to hurt anybody," number three whispered. "We aren't, right?"

Micah mentally noted that number three was a girl, and by the way, she carried herself, she was only a girl. Probably a teenager.

"We've already hurt someone; or did you not notice the dead security guard,' scoffed number four.

"We wait until…"

"Hold on." Micah saw number four hold up a finger and look towards him. He pretended to have his eyes scanning the area. When he dared look back again, the four of them had moved far enough away from him to make out the words.

The girl who had been collecting electronics was

staring at him. She was probably wondering when he was going to man up and save the day, and Eli wasn't helping.

"Look at these people around us," Eli whispered. "Someone is gonna crack and do something stupid."

"Besides you? What are you doing here?"

"It's a bank. I need money like everybody else. Trust me; I have better things to do than sit here under the gun of some inexperienced criminals."

"More people to torture?" Micah growled. "I swear that you aren't going to get out of here a free man."

"You should probably work on us getting out of here period. I sense a problem coming up very soon."

Micah scanned the hostages. Nervous looks. Shifty eyes. Thought processes working over time. It wasn't easy realizing that you were in a situation like this. Micah stopped looking. Sure enough, they weren't the only ones having conversations. Three of the bank workers were seated together. Mouths were barely moving, but they were definitely planning something.

Number four stepped back in front of the group with number one. They both had chairs and sat down facing the group.

"All right, people. Hopefully, the cops outside do what they need to do, and you'll all be outta here in time for a late lunch."

"You don't need all of these hostages, you know. The more hostages, the more attention." Micah groaned. He wasn't sure if it was a manager or just one of those personal bankers, but the guy was probably spouting off something he saw on a TV show. *Please, stop,* Micah thought to himself. Number four turned his attention to the man.

"And you are an expert in hostages situations? You want to tell me my options?"

The banker stood up slowly. "Just let the customers go. It shows that you aren't here to hurt anyone, and the workers here will cooperate with you fully. I promise."

Number four and number two laughed to each other. "I tell you what. How about you sit down and shut up, and I won't send you out like I sent that security guard."

The banker didn't sit. Instead, he kept his hands visible but continued to talk. "Come on. You obviously are just caught up in a bad situation. You don't want to hurt anybody else, and it isn't too late to…"

Micah jolted when the gunshot sounded. He started to reach for his, but Eli's hand stopped him. Number four had just fired into the wall above the banker who dropped back down the ground immediately. Several screams and cried echoed in the bank. Number two and three looked back from where they were but didn't seem too rattled. Number four addressed the group.

"Listen. This man is right. We don't want to hurt anyone else, but if we have to, we will not hesitate. We've got nothing to lose. Do you?" There were no responses. Eli removed his hand, and Micah relaxed. Number four lowered his gun. "Good. Now stay seated and shut up!"

CHAPTER THREE

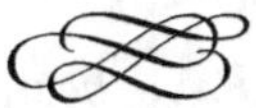

The gunshot caused a brief few seconds of silence where everyone started to think the worst. Ailani quickly began to order his men to move any bystanders away from the area. Reporters were busy addressing cameramen. Raine stood by Tai as they were reading the information on the laptop in front of them. If it weren't for the few sentences she had read, panic wouldn't have been the first resort.

"Tink dey shot sumbody?" Tai asked.

"I don't know," Raine said. "We need to find this stuff, Tai. Whatever they need this serum for, I'm pretty sure that they are willing to do anything to get it."

Nothing showed up when they searched for that particular serum, but a lot populated when they searched Commander Walt Painter. Raine stared at the words 'decorated,' 'honored,' 'revered,' and knew that this man was not just some average Joe. What caught her eye were several articles about Victor Painter, his son. *The tumor is located at the base of the brain stem. The placement of the tumor along with the rapid growth in the past few months has increased the likelihood that this cancer cannot be stopped. All attempts to slow down the progression have been futile.* Raine saw Ailani walking towards her.

"I've got SWAT on their way just in case," he said. "Tell me that you've got something."

"Tai and I need to go to Tripler," she said. "I have a feeling that whatever this serum is that it won't be easy to get. Tell them that I'm on it though."

Ailani frowned as she nodded to the phone in his hand. "You're going to leave me with this, huh. I brought you here for this, you know."

Raine knew. She also didn't want to admit that knowing Micah was in the bank, too, was causing a little more than just a twinge of anxiety. She needed something else to occupy her mind and finding the serum so that she could prevent any harm to the people inside the bank was the only option.

Ailani held the phone to his ear as he watched the two of them go.

"Yeah," was the answer.

"This is Officer Ailani Kimo Kaihale. I'm the officer in charge out front."

"What happened to the woman? The doctor?"

"She's gonna see if she can find your serum. We are trying to make sure we help everybody in there including you. We heard a shot out here. Just want to make sure no one is hurt."

"Nobody's hurt," the man said gruffly. "We just needed to establish the roles in here. As long as everyone cooperates, it'll stay that way."

"So, nobody is hurt at all?" Ailani pressed. "We also have witnesses saying there was a shot when the bank was first taken over."

There was a brief pause. Then, "Like I said. None of the hostages are hurt."

Ailani knew there was a lie in there somehow. He took a deep breath and spoke. "Listen, I'm your man out here. We are going to get your serum, but it may take a little longer than sixty minutes, okay."

Click. Ailani, squeeze the device hard as he brought it away from his ear.

* * *

RAINE CLOSED the phone slowly and brought it to her lips in thought. Tai looked over at her.

"Wat dey say?"

"No such thing," Raine said. "R33PM doesn't exist in any records in the hospital. They do, however, have Victor Painter as a patient there, but they couldn't give me information."

"We gon see wen we get der," Tai said confidently. "Kahi malaila O kekahi e loa'a O ke ala. Where there is a will, there is a way."

"You're so inspirational, Tai," Raine laughed.

"You worried bout Micah?"

"More than I'd like to admit." They had been allowing this facade of friendship to play out without addressing some key things in their life. As much as she wanted to start over again. She knew that she couldn't as long as Eli Samuels was out there wanting to ruin her life.

"Micah knows wat he's doin'," Tai said whipping his steering wheel from side to side dodging traffic. He drove like a maniac with the calmness of a guru. "No worries."

They arrived at Tripler main gate, and Tai made sure that he kept the flashing lights on when he pulled up.

"What's the emergency?" The officer at the main gate asked.

"I'm Lieutenant Tai Ulafala, MP," Tai produced his ID. "We got an emergency that got to do wit a bank robbery downtown."

"We need to get a hold of the doctor who is taking care of a patient here, and we need to do it fast," Raine leaned over the center console of the truck.

The guard looked at them strangely but went back inside of his post. Within a moment, he leaned back out and nodded to them.

"You'll go up to Neurology. Fourth floor. Wing C. Someone will meet you there."

When the guard gave the okay, Tai floored the gas pedal sending the truck into a squeal. Raine glanced at her watch as they jumped out of the car, and ran into the Oceanside entrance of the center. They had made it there with forty-three minutes to spare. They kept their badges out for anyone who gave them a suspicious look, and Raine was very aware that her shorts and tank top combo didn't scream authority. Neither did Tai's Hawaiin shirt and khakis. *All of this military is making me think about Micah again. C'mon, Raine, there is nothing wrong. You're about to save the day.*

When the elevator opened up on the fourth floor, they were greeted by several uniforms. Raine could tell by their demeanor that they were not going to deliver good news.

"Lieutenant Ulafala, I presume." An older gentleman looked Tai in the eye; briefly glancing at his wardrobe.

"Yes, sir. And dis is Doctor Raine Michelson of HPD. We here lookin' fo..."

"My name is Colonel Roger Edison. I am the personal doctor for Commander Painter and his family. I'm sorry to stop you here, but we aren't able to help you with your search."

"What do you mean you can't help us?" Raine frowned.

"I mean that I can't help you. We received your calls about a serum, and there is no such serum. Wherever you got your intel, they were wrong."

Raine glared at the men accompanying him. She cleared her throat and offered a small smile. "Colonel Edison, there are several hostages being held at gunpoint in a bank downtown. The men holding them specifically mentioned R33PM and Commander Painter."

"Miss, if I'm hearing correct, then you are searching for something based off the word of criminals."

"Criminals who mention Commander Painter by name," Raine said. "Any reason why they would equate the two?"

"Commander Painter is a decorated officer. I'm sure the list of people who know of him is very deep," He nodded to them. "I don't want to waste your time, and I do have a lot of work to…"

"Sir, no disrespect, but someting don't smell right," Tai scowled. "You sayin day you know nutin bout dat serum? Lives are at stake."

"Yes, they are," Edison said. "Everyday. Excuse me."

Raine felt a burning anger boiling in her as he left and the soldiers that accompanied him stood by watching them. Tai swore out loud, and Raine put a hand on his shoulder. "Calm down, Tai. We are going to figure this out." Tai grunted but pulled out his cell phone. He stepped away, but the eyes of the soldiers followed him. As much as the Colonel was trying to disparage their search by discrediting the source, the fact that he met them at the elevator and did not want them going further suggested that there was something there.

A doctor appeared from around the corner holding some folders. She glanced briefly at the soldiers, but only gave a nod which was returned. Passing by Raine on the way to the elevator, the doctor whispered, "come with me."

Raine didn't turn right away but waited until she heard the elevator open before turning around to see the doctor nodding at her.

"Tai, come," Raine said stepping into the elevator. Tai followed while still on the phone. "Wat do you mean we can't talk to him?" Tai's frustration was growing. Raine rarely saw this side of him. She never saw him angry. Frustrated. Concerned. Never angry. Tai hung up the phone and noticed that he and Raine weren't the only ones in the elevator.

"Who dis?" Tai said.

"My name is Healani. I'm a med student. I overheard what you were talking about with Colonel Edison. He's been informed since you first called that someone was coming here to look for R33PM."

"You've heard of that? The serum?" Raine asked. Healani nodded.

"Not only that, I know who created the serum." The elevator door opened, and Healani put a finger to her lips. She walked out of the elevator, and the two of them followed a few feet behind. Raine felt her heart pounding as she realized that Healani's revelation immediately made things more complicated. Now, instead of the men in the bank being wrong and confronted about it; they were right and going to be pissed about why they weren't getting it— whatever it was.

"What is R33PM, Healani?" Raine asked as they sat in an empty waiting room at the far end of another wing.

"It's a virus," the girl said. "I can only tell you what I know. I don't know them personally, but several months ago, three medical students were working on a project that would help with easing PTSD in officers in the field. Every trial seemed to just set them back farther in their research. Apparently, they were using different animals that they had been subjected to traumatic experiences and studying the effects on the brain when they discovered one of the animals had a tumor. The serum that they made—completely eliminated the tumor. No trace."

Raine closed her eyes. "Victor Painter."

Healani held up the folder in her hands. "He has a tumor on his brain stem, and it's forming an aneurysm on top of it."

"How dis serum stuff get to da Commander," Tai asked.

"Well, when something this big happens, you got to be careful who you trust with the information. They must have told the wrong people," Healani shrugged. "I know that there are several instructors who would have been the first to know about the projects, but everyone knows Commander Painter."

"So, the serum is under lockdown because Painter wants it for his son? Are you serious? How can one man prevent us from saving lives?"

"Because while it works against the tumor, it is also a virus, and there is no telling what it can do in the wrong hands," Healani handed Raine the folder. "Listen, I've got to get back. If you really want to know what happened, you need to talk to one of the students who created it."

"They here?" Tai asked.

"No. No." Healani stood. "They all kinda of disappeared off the face of the earth. That folder has their names and files though. Hopefully, that helps you find them."

When the girl left, Raine slammed the folder on the seat next to them. They didn't have time for this, but she also knew that wasn't going to get anywhere as a civilian—no matter what her position was.

"We shud call Ailani," Tai said grabbing his phone. Raine nodded. Ailani was probably pulling his hair out. They had thirty minutes left.

I've got to get more from these guys, she thought. Tai was standing with his back towards her, and Raine knew that Ailani was trying to make sense of what Tai was telling him. She grabbed her phone and found the number she was looking for.

"Hello?"

"It's Dr. Raine Michelson. Are you the one I talked to earlier?"

"I am. What happened to the man? What the hell are you planning? I told you what we wanted."

"I know," Raine said calmly. "I know. I'm working on getting it, but I need your help. Why are you looking for this serum? Why do you need it?"

"That's not important. You just get it to us. Time is running out."

"Listen to me," Raine said firmly. "If you know that Commander Painter has the serum, then you know why and why he won't give it up. I need your help here."

There was silence on the other line. Raine closed her eyes in frustration. *Think, Raine. Think.*

"I know that you have put yourself in an impossible place and that you have done it for a good reason," she said softly. "You aren't criminals. I could tell. For some reason, you saw no other way than to do what you're doing now. I get it. I also know that you need me to get this serum for you. I am the best option you have. Trust me."

There. That had to be vulnerable enough to elicit the right response. Silence still echoed over the line, and Tai seemed to be wrapping up his conversation with Ailani.

"Caroline Mays." That was it. The line disconnected.

"Who wuz dat?" Tai asked.

"It was information. C'mon, we need to find out where these kids are." She said grabbing the folder from the chair. The best option was to make headway and then ask for more time. Raine felt like she could get it if she played her cards right. Hopefully, Micah was playing his right inside the bank.

* * *

THE MASK WAS SUFFOCATING. The bank was suffocating. For the first time, she understood what claustrophobia felt like. It was scary. Though her eyes could see that she had enough space and air to breathe, her mind was telling her something different. It was telling her that this was the end.

There was an office out of sight of the other hostages and away from the windows that Macy could crouch down against the desk, placed the gun on the floor, and stripped off her mask. With the stripping of the mask came the tears —tears that had paused from the night before and now felt the freedom to fall. Before that, they had sprung a lot. Sometimes, she felt like the only one who cried though she knew that the others did, too.

Macy swallowed hard as she closed her eyes. It wasn't easy to do that these days. The only images that she saw were those of her mother's body lying on the hospital bed with machines beeping and monitoring every single signal that the woman was still alive. The tumor had caught them off guard. Adam had been the one to find his mom on the floor of the kitchen when he had stopped by during a lunch break to pick up something from home. Macy had been called out of class and Bryce had picked her up to take her to the hospital. The tumor had developed on the brain stem, and it was too dangerous to operate at that point in time. Chemotherapy was an option, but they weren't wealthy. They barely had enough money to cover what hospital bills that were already piling up. Macy and Adam found whatever jobs they could to help, but they needed some sort of miracle. That's when Bryce had a breakthrough.

He had met her while stationed in Hawaii. They had actually almost dated but decided that only being friends was a better option.

"Bryce, I have something! I have something big!"

"Palila, you sound crazy. What's going on? You've been blowing up my phone all day?"

"I told you that I've been working on a project to help with PTSD," she said rapidly. "We failed spectacularly at that, but I think we found something better, and I think it can help your mom!"

Palila told Bryce that no one, but the group she worked with knew about the serum—yet. It was experimental and not something they could legally say was a cure for anything, but—it had worked. For a couple of weeks, Bryce had been filled in about more experiments and tests, and he had relayed everything to them. Palila planned to sneak some of the serum out before they actually turned in their findings. A plane ticket had been purchased for her. They had made plans to get her into the hospital. There was hope. Palila never got on the plane.

Macy jumped when a masked-covered face appeared from over the desk. "What the hell are you doing? Put your mask back on!"

Macy squeezed the balled-up mask in her hands. "No one can see me. I couldn't breathe in that thing."

"I don't care!"

"We killed someone though," she said softly, shuddering at the thought of the security guard. "No, I killed someone.

"Adam squatted beside her. "Listen, little sister, Dad and Bryce weren't going to let you come on this thing. They wanted you to stay home. I'm the one that said you should come because you are a part of this family, and this is all for our family."

"I know." Macy's gaze dropped to the floor.

"You know? Do you remember how mom looked when we last saw her? She's barely alive. We have to do whatever it takes to get that damn prick's attention, and we need to get that serum."

"I know," Macy growled. Adam sighed.

"Then snap out of this. Put your mask on."

Macy did what she was told and followed her brother out of the office. The hostages looked exhausted from the stress of the situation. There were a few bank workers, a mother and her daughter who was probably only a couple years younger than Macy, and several randoms. Two men sat against the back wall. They whispered to each other periodically, but other than that, were quiet.

"You haven't said anything lately," Micah muttered. Eli had stretched out his legs and leaned his head back against the wall with a relaxed look on his face.

"What do you want me to say? It sounds like we're waiting for your friends out there to break up this party, and they're too scared to do anything. Kind of like you are too scared to do something."

"There are people in…"

"Just like you are scared to admit that I'm right about Raine."

"Don't talk about her," Micah growled. Eli shrugged.

"No worries. If you don't want to face the truth, then don't."

"You don't know anything about truth. Your truth is warped."

"Raine doesn't deserve your love just like her fiancé didn't either. What is with you idiots falling in love with these women who cheat on you, treat you like dirt, and make you weak."

Micah clenched his mouth shut and waited for a few seconds before addressing the last comment. "Is that what happened to you? You were so hurt by Raine that you had to see her destroyed. How does it feel to know that it isn't working?" This time Eli was silent. His jaw flexed as he crossed his arms across his waist. Movement from across the group caught Micah's attention. The same banker that had tried to reason with the gunmen before stood up. Gunman number four looked up with some interest and tilted his gun up towards the man.

"I suggest you sit back down, sir. I won't ask you a second time."

"Please," the banker held up his hands. "I know that you

aren't killers. The guard was an accident. We can tell them that."

Number three was very quiet. Number two had pulled her out of one of the offices earlier where she was obviously hiding. If she was getting overwhelmed, then maybe there was a way to get the others to unravel, too.

Number four stood up from his seat and pointed the gun to a woman who sat only a few away from him. The barrel aimed at her head.

"You've got ten seconds. Either you take a seat now, or she takes a seat permanently, and then we will see who isn't a killer."

It was plain to see that the banker wanted to challenge this proposition, but the fear in the woman's eyes dissuaded him. Micah sighed. Something was going to go down soon, and he had the feeling that he was going to have to decide on how it all played out.

CHAPTER FOUR

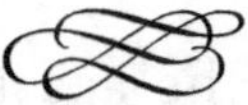

Time was not on their side, and that made Raine a little nervous. Out of the three names that Healani had given them, they were only able to find information on one of them. Rafael Puluka had an address in Mililani. Normally, it took twenty minutes to get there from where they were, but Tai made it in half the time. Raine had spent her time on the phone trying to get someone to track where Rafael would be at that time as well as trying to keep Ailani in the loop.

The apartment complexed barely looked livable. For a military medical student, the kid was not living the high life. According to the papers that were in the folder, Rafael along with two others, Palila and Philip, were top students as well as soldiers, all of them were specializing in

Neurology. They were members of a few clinical trials. There was nothing that mentioned R33PM.

"How you wanna do dis?" Tia asked as they pulled up. "Good cop, bad cop? Two bad cops?"

"Whatever you want, Tai," Raine said. "As long as we get the information."

Something stirred in the apartment when Tia's meaty fist banged on the door. The footsteps were light. Obviously, someone was trying to sneak up to the door as to not make it seems like they were there. Raine pushed Tai out of the way and stood in front of the peephole. She heard light scuffling on the door and smiled.

"Who is it?"

"I'm looking for Rafael Puluka. Is he here?"

"Doesn't live here anymore. Goodbye."

"Please," Raine said. "It's an emergency."

No answer. Raine looked at Tai and nodded to the door. Tai smiled. He was bad cop. He only needed a few steps momentum to ram into the door and snapped the frame by the lock. The door swung open, and Raine stared at the wide-eyed, boy standing in his boxers and t-shirt with a glass in his hand. For a second, they stared at him, and he at them. Then, Raine saw something on the table in between them and him. It was a gun.

"Rafael?" Raine started. That seemed to jump start him again, and he dropped the glass. He moved with lightning speed towards the gun, and Raine dove for it at the exact same time. Her fingers grasped at it but missed as he snatched it and rolled to the side pulling it up and pointing it at her as she sat on her knees.

"Hold on, brudda," Tai's voice boomed. Out of her peripheral, she noticed that Tai had his gun trained on the boy.

"Put your gun down, or I blow her brains out. Don't think that I won't." Panic was written all over Rafael's face. This kid was terrified.

"Rafael," she said softly, holding up her hands. "I don't want you to be afraid. My name is Raine, and the big guy over there is Tai."

"Don't give a damn," Rafael's voice trembled. "You won't kill me. You're not getting me, too."

"We don't want to kill you," Raine said. "I'm with HPD, and he's is military police. We've come here for your help."

"Shit!" He adjusted his fingers on the gun and glanced at Tai. "Neither of you look like cops."

"We're here because there is an emergency, and we don't have a lot of time." She lowered her hands. "Now, my partner here is going to lower his gun, and we hope that you will lower yours, too. I'll show you my credentials."

Tai sighed but lowered his gun. Rafael stood up from his position and backed away from both of them. Raine turned around on her knees and made sure he could see that she was pulling her identification out of her back pocket. She held it out, and he quickly grabbed it.

"Fine, so it says that you're a cop." He tossed it back. "Doesn't mean anything."

"We ain't got time fo you to feel safe," Tai said. "We got people who need you? You know der is a bank hold up."

"Saw something on the news? What's that got to do with me?"

"The robbers don't want money. They want R33PM." The gun in his hand that started to lower was raised up again.

"Who sent you? Was it Painter? Was it!"

"No, Rafael. We are trying to find this serum? We know that you and your friends created it, and somehow they took it from you."

"Took it?" Rafael laughed spitefully. "Is that what you heard? They didn't take it; they ordered us to give it to them. When we questioned them, they-they destroyed us."

"Talk to me," Raine said. "We can help you, but we need to know what's going on here."

Rafael lowered the gun, but keep it in his hand. He leaned against the wall and shook his head.

"I don't know if you can help. We knew that we couldn't sit on R33PM and not reveal our findings. Our clinical trials are monitored by our department heads. So, we had to bring our information to him."

"I'm guessing that Colonel Edison is your department head?" Rafael nodded.

"Before we brought it to him, Palila said that she wanted to take some to her friend in the States to help with his mom's tumor. Philip and I freaked out on her. We hadn't tested the serum on a real medical situation, and legally, it was against every protocol we were supposed to do. If the serum turned out to be lethal to the woman or caused something else, then we were liable. We didn't want that to happen."

"So, you told Edison," Tai said. "Then what? C'mon, time is tickin'."

"Edison wanted to see it for himself. He wanted to experiment with it. Then he started bringing Commander Painter down to our lab. Soon, he was excluding us from any conversations about the project. Finally, we were given orders that our project had been canceled per order Colonel Edison. We were all furious, but Palila was more. She went to Edison's office, and I'm not sure what she said, but the next day when we tried to get to the lab to at least get our work, we couldn't. There were soldiers blocking us from going any further."

"They took it over."

Rafael nodded. "Yeah, at least the thought they did. Palila figured that Edison would pull something, and she grabbed all of the plans and as much of the serum as she could before they closed us all out."

"So, she has the serum, too!" Tai said. "Great. How we get in touch wit her?"

Rafael snorted. "You think that I pulled this gun on you just for kicks? Palila is dead. They killed her, and they're trying to kill me, too."

Raine shook her head. "You're telling me that Colonel Edison killed Palila and is trying to kill you and Philip?"

"It goes beyond Edison. It's got to be Painter. And I haven't heard from Philip in days, so I'm assuming that either he is hiding or—dead. See, they never found the plans or serum that Palila kept. She hid them somewhere. We had nowhere to go because Edison put it out that we had stolen stuff from Tripler, and we were being searched for. When I heard what happened to Palila, I knew something was going down. I got this place, and I pulled as much money as I could out of the bank. I'm trying to lay low, and then go back to the States, and live with my cousin for a bit."

Raine looked at Tai. An hour was almost up. She needed to stall for time with the gunmen and with Ailani. This case had just escalated even more.

* * *

"YOU THINK I'M A FOOL, don't you! I don't like being played for a fool. If you don't think this is serious, I will prove that to you."

Macy didn't like how her dad sounded on the phone. He was a gentleman normally and rarely acted out in anger. Well, he had been angry a lot, and that had become the new normal. His face was red now, and his body shook so much that he clinched the phone tight in his grip just so that he could focus his anger on something.

"Why should I trust you!" Bryce sat watching the hostages, and Adam now watched what was going on outside. Macy was scared to death to look. In here, they had the guns. Out there, a lot of cops were ready to shoot them on sight, and they still didn't know that someone was dead. It was hard to think about, and she really didn't want to imagine the consequences. They needed the serum to save their mother's life. That was all.

Her father slammed the phone down. The boys walked over to him while keeping their eyes on the hostages.

"What happened?" Bryce asked. Macy watched as her father closed his eyes, the face mask covering the full expression on his face.

"They want more time," he said. Bryce and Adam both started to protest, but he cut them off. "The woman from earlier says that she is going to find that serum, but she needs to find out where it's hidden. At least, that's what the cop from outside said. He assures me that they won't move on us as long as we promise not to hurt anyone."

"And what makes you think that they're going to honor that promise?" Adam asked. His father sighed and then looked back at Bryce.

"They mentioned Palila."

Bryce clenched his teeth and shook his head. "How much time?"

"Another hour. She will call us personally."

Micah leaned back with his head on the wall. He was trying to think of a plan. The bank wasn't that big. There was only one front door, and he assumed a backdoor or exit. Maybe someone had to go to the bathroom. They had been in this place for over an hour, and no one had to go? Eli mimicked his position.

"Whatever the police are getting for them seems to be a big deal," he whispered. "Kind surprised they haven't taken these four right now."

"I know you don't really care about others, but the police do."

"You automatically assume that I don't care about others, Lieutenant. I feel like that is an unfair judgment."

Micah snorted. "Unfair, huh? You have done everything that you've done because you are upset that Raine made mistakes, that she isn't perfect. That someone could see past that and love her despite her failures. That's what this whole vendetta is based on, and you've ruined lives because of it."

Eli shrugged. "That's what everything is based on, Lieutenant. Don't you see that?"

"You're delusional."

"Right, let me ask you a question then?" Micah groaned inside. "You have the choice of choosing whether to shoot that girl over there who picked up our phones or the girl that's with the gunmen. Who do you choose?"

"That's a stupid question."

"No, it isn't. Both girls are so young and impressionable, but if you had the choice between saving one or the other, you would choose the girl who is the hostage even though you have no idea of the story behind the girl who is the criminal."

"She is a criminal. She has consequences for her actions no matter what she did. I can't ignore that fact."

"See, now you sound like me. Whatever has this girl in the situation that she is in, you have already decided that she deserves judgment. It doesn't matter. She's failed."

Micah noticed some movement to the far side of him and watched as the banker who had constantly been challenging the gunmen was moving in front of the group quickly towards him. Micah scooted into Eli who grunted a cuss word in his direction. The banker slid in beside Micah, who saw him looked down to the side of the person next to him.

"So, the little girl was right? You're a cop?" Micah's eyes grew wide, and he glared at Eli as if to say *This is your fault.* "Why haven't you done anything yet?"

"Because the time isn't right, and we need to let the cops do what they're supposed to do."

The banker nodded slowly. Micah suddenly felt very uneasy. He didn't like the fact that more people knew about him being a cop, and if the banker and girl knew, more did also.

"I'm Ted, by the way." Micah didn't feel like introducing himself at all, but Eli stuck his arm right in front of him and shook the banker's hand.

"The name is Eli. Good to meet you."

What do they think this is? A committee meeting?

"Hey!" Ted called out. "Can I get my inhaler? It's in the desk in the office up front."

Number four stared at the banker for a while before answering. "You don't look like you need it."

"You should probably think about getting it. You don't want a situation where this guy has a panic attack and dies," Eli chipped in. "Then you've got two dead ones on your hands."

Number four snarled, and then nodded towards number three, who disappeared for a moment before returning with a small inhaler. She stepped in front of the banker.

Micah wasn't sure when it had happened, but the gun that he had been trying to hide found its way into the Ted's hands. The inhaler dropped to the ground as the man bounded to his feet and grabbed number three. He twirled her around and wrapped one arm around her neck with the gun quickly pointed at her temple. The hostages in the building sensed immediately that the escalation was not good. Number four jumped up from his seat and pointed his gun at the banker.

"Put the gun down!" Ted said. "Put it down!"

"You have made a serious mistake, man. Serious!" The commotion caused the other two to come from where they were standing and pause at the scene before them. Ted tightened his grip around the girl. "Put your guns down! Now! Or she dies!"

Micah watched along with Eli as Number two quickly put his gun up and pointed it at the little girl with her mom. *Dammit! You fool!*" Number two took several steps and picked up the girl by her hair as she screamed. He put her in a similar hold to what the banker had Number three.

"You let her go, sir, and I won't ask a second time."

Micah wasn't sure why the conversation entered his mind at that time other than he saw the process that Eli was thinking. There were two girls. Two innocent girls, and if something didn't change, then both were going to die. Not one of them, but both. He couldn't choose, but he didn't have to choose.

Ted looked trapped. Micah couldn't see the faces behind the masks, but he bet that they felt the same way. He stood up slowly.

"Hey, let's calm down here," he said.

"Sit down," Number one said to him. "You don't want to be in the line of fire. Cause the banker has gotten on my last nerve."

"Just let me say something," Micah said. "I—I'm a cop."

Number four pointed his gun at Micah now, and the barrel of it seemed gigantic with vulnerable. "It's my gun. Let me fix this." Micah kept his hands visible, and his eyes unwavering to number one. "Ted put down the gun."

The banker gasped. "You're out of your mind!"

"Put the gun down! Let the girl go!"

"I do that, and they kill me. They kill us both."

"They won't. Because they are here for something, and they haven't gotten it yet. What they are here for is not your life."

"I'm not letting her go. They need to put their...." Micah turned to Ted.

"We don't know the story, and we can't act on rash judgments. We've got to trust that the police can handle it. Just do us all a favor and shut the hell up."

Ted's eyes were full of fury and fear. He looked back and forth from Micah to the gunmen. Finally, he slowly released his grip on the girl. She glanced at Micah, and for the first time, he saw her eyes. *Dear God, she's just a kid. There's hurt there.* Number three quickly moved away from the banker, and Micah slowly took the gun from him, too.

"Hold on there," Number one cautioned. Micah put the safety back on the gun, took a step forward, and offered it to the man.

"Just let the girl go, and we will go back to sitting here patiently."

"He's bluffing," Number four said. Micah stood completely still, hoping that he was right about these men. Number one took several slow steps and grabbed the gun. Micah released it. They stood there for a moment before number one said, "Let the girl go."

Number two let her go trembling back to her spot with her mother. Micah nodded to number one and sat back down. Eli leaned over to him once everything had calmed a bit.

"Not sure if that was the smartest thing or the dumbest, but..."

"But," Micah interrupted, "I answered your question.

None of them have to die. The one who is innocent and the one who is guilty can both live. Therefore, the one who loves without failure and the one who falls in love can both live as well."

Eli stared at him silently. Micah knew that he had won that round.

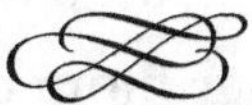

CHAPTER FIVE

"She was staying here? Right here?"

Raine raised an eyebrow. Rafael had basically hid out in the worst place possible hoping that no one would find him. Palila had chosen a place a little different. A number of kids played in the yard in front of the building. They were all under the age of ten and looked to not have a care in the world. The house wasn't a palace, but it was nice and well-kept. It looked like it had been built decades around and been updated on several occasions.

"What is this place?"

"A foster home," Rafael said as the three of them stood on the sidewalk. "Palila grew up in it, and she never left. She said that the kids she grew up with were the reason that she joined the military and wanted to become a medic. A lot of the kids lost parents who were in active duty or because of something that happened to a parent who was married to someone in the military. She wanted to help soldiers overcome adversities so that they could be there for their family. Actually, she just wanted to help people period."

"You know how she ended up here?" Tai asked. "Her dad was killed overseas, and her mom died of cancer."

Raine sighed. Things were starting to make sense now. The question was how did she die. When she took the research, what happened next and how did it get back into Edison and Painter's hands?

"So, she lived in the house?" Raine asked. Rafael shook his head.

"In a trailer in the back." He pointed to them. "You guys start to head around, and I'm going to tell Mrs. Pau what's going on. She's the foster mom, and she's been pretty paranoid since—well—since it happened."

Rafael jogged up to the door, and they started to walk around the house. Sure enough, there was a trailer. It looked somewhat nice as well as far as trailers go. The outside was a dingy, off-white, but it was also spotless. The windows were blocked with curtains, and a small Honda Accord sat off to the side.

The door was unlocked, and Raine stepped into the cleanest area, she had ever seen. Palila had been in medicine, but what Raine had expected to see in the trailer wasn't what she saw. There was a small living room with a huge map plastered to the wall with small magnetic strips to pinpoint certain places that Raine assumed, she had traveled to or wanted to travel to. There was a small, blue couch with a colorful blanket draped over it. The end table in front of it held a single picture of a man and woman. It was old.

"Her parents?" Tai asked picking it up. Raine nodded.

The kitchen was spotless. Only one dish lay in the sink, and it looked to have last held cereal. Throughout the rest of the house were pictures of her and the kids or pictures of her and other soldiers. She had a lot of them. She was not only proud of her work, but she was proud of the people that she helped.

The front door opened, and Rafael entered the trailer. "Did you see the room yet? Mrs. Pau said that the police combed through it, but it's pretty much the same as it was when she was found."

"How was she killed?" Raine asked as she walked back through the small hallway towards the bedroom.

"Strangled."

The room was a mess. The bed was broken and sunk to the ground. A small bookshelf had been turned over, and books were scattered everywhere. There were a few papers on the floor, but none of them looked like anything scientific. Just some financial papers and banking information. Raine put her hands on her hips. The trailer wasn't that big. There was no way she would have brought the stuff back here and tried to hide it.

"Rafael," Raine asked. "Do you know who found her?"

He shook his head. "I didn't ask a lot of questions when I found out. A lot happened. I shouldn't even be out here like this."

"Tai, can you get a copy of the medical examiner's report on her. Like ASAP?" Tai nodded and waddled out of the trailer. Raine sighed. *A young medical officer is working on a serum to help with PTSD and comes across something that destroys tumors. She wants to use it to help a friend but is told she had to give it up to save another. She is told that it is a virus that could be used for evil, but she just needed enough to save a woman's life.*

She had already put together that whoever was asking for the serum in that bank was associated with Palila's friend's mom or was actually her friend come to collect on the serum. If they knew that Painter was a part of this, then Palila must have told them.

"So why take hostages unless they knew she was dead and knew Painter had the serum?" She thought the last part aloud.

Raine turned around in the room. Suddenly, her eyes widened. Rafael stared at her strangely.

"You've got this weird looking in your eyes. Did you figure something out?"

"Maybe," Raine said leaving the bedroom. "Maybe."

Tai gave her a funny look from his truck as she was on the phone and his computer at the same time. Rafael followed closely behind her as she walked directly to the house in front.

"Wait, what are you doing?" Rafael asked jogging to stay in front of her. "Mrs. Pau doesn't like people just walking into her house."

"She's going to love me." Raine kept walking and two the porch steps two at a time. She knocked on the door loudly and waited with Rafael glaring at her.

Mrs. Pau was a short, stout woman with long dark hair and native Hawaiian features. She looked at Raine, and then Rafael.

"Whut chu want?" The question was asked with suspicion, and Raine gave her a sympathetic smile.

"Mrs. Pau, my name is Raine, and I'm just getting to know Palila. I'm so sorry for your loss." Mrs. Pau nodded. "She loved these kids, didn't she?"

"Dey love her. She stayed up with them when they sick. She always brings dem gifts. She like dey big sista."

"So Palila dedicated her life to the military and these kids. No men in her life?"

Mrs. Pau smirked. "Palila did not like men. Men liked her. She neva bring dem around. Only one."

"What was his name?"

"Bryce. She talked bout him like dey wuz best fraands? I tink he liked her, but she neva let it go far. Why you askin'?"

"Because I think that Bryce is in trouble, and he doesn't have to be," Raine sighed. "One more thing, Mrs. Pau. Who found the body?"

Mrs. Pau looked down at the ground. "I did. Glad it not

one a da kids. She ain't come to break fuss, and I saw dat her car wuz by da trailer. I ain't see it in da driveway like usual."

"Thank you, Mrs. Pau. You have helped beyond what I could have asked for, and thank you for what you do for these kids."

She gave Mrs. Pau a hug and ushered Rafael out. "What's going on?" He asked confused.

"I've figured it out," Raine said. She jogged over to the truck where Tai was just finishing up a phone call.

"Eh, so I got da info from the medical examiner," Tai said. "She was strangled. Dey think dat it was by a strap or a belt."

"They're right. It was from a belt," Raine said. "I noticed something when we pulled up. Everything is clean. Mrs. Pau raises these kids to keep things nice and tidy. She raised Palila that way. Palila is the epitome of nice and tidy. Her trailer proves that. So, why would she park her car on the grass behind the house?"

"She wouldn't," Rafael said.

"You're right," Raine pointed to the grass. "If that were a habit of hers, the grass would be worn from all of the times that she drove on it. She didn't park her car by the trailer."

"Wait," Tai frowned. "You saying someone moved da car der?"

"Someone who knew that she lived in the trailer. Someone who strangled her and killed her but not in her trailer. If someone had come to the trailer to kill her, there would have been more damage to the front of the trailer. If there was a struggle enough to break the bed and turnover a bookcase, there would have been a struggle near the door. Tai, you said the report says she was strangled with a belt. Could it have been a seat belt?"

Tai looked over the documents that were faxed over on his screen. "Damn. I tink it could of."

Rafael held up his hands. "Wait. So someone strangled her in her car and then drove her body to her place and messed up her bedroom and left her there? Why?"

" I have my theory, but I don't have time to share it," Raine looked at her watch. "I need a moment alone."

She walked down the sidewalk several yards leaving the two of them to go back to the trailer and car. Raine took out her phone and dialed the recent number.

"What."

"Hello, again. This is Dr. Michelson and…"

"Do you have the serum?"

"I don't," Raine said softly. She heard the man began to gear up; so, she spoke again quickly.

"I need to talk to Bryce."

There was a pause. Then, "I don't know what you're talking about."

"I know that Bryce is there. Put him on the phone, and I'll tell you where the serum is."

"You just said you didn't have it."

Raine kicked at the ground with her toe. "I don't. Didn't say I didn't know where it was though."

There was a pause on the phone.

Bryce looked at his father. The man pulled the receiver away from his ear and looked at him.

"She wants to talk to you." Bryce raised an eyebrow. *Why him?* He stared at the phone for a moment. "C'mon, she said she knows where the serum is."

Bryce took the phone and placed it to his ear. "What do you want?"

"I want you to tell me about what happened when you last went to Palila's trailer, Bryce. What happened?"

$$* * *$$

BRYCE TOOK a sip of his drink while he waited at the stop light. He wasn't a huge fan of soda, but he was exhausted. Well, beyond exhausted. The flight from Hawaii had been so last minute that he hadn't had the time to prepare for it. The day before he had spent at the hospital, running errands, meetings with his command, and the securing the flight. Palila had called him late in the day.

"What happened!" Bryce had answered immediately after seeing her name pop up on the caller ID. "I waited for you at the airport a couple of days ago. I tried calling you. I tried texting and emailing you."

"I'm sorry, Bryce," Palila said. "There's been a setback."

Bryce felt his heart almost stop. There couldn't be any setbacks. This was the only hope they had for his mother right now. "What do you mean?"

"They want the serum. Our superiors, Commander Painter and Colonel Edison. They want to take everything."

"This is my mom's only hope right now, Pae! You said you could get us something."

"And I can! I promise. I just need you to get here." Bryce groaned. "I have to have you come—I—I'm not safe right now."

"Why?"

"Yesterday I found out one of the reasons why they want the serum. Commander Painter's son has cancer. Colonel Edison told me that he was going to take over the research. He's already got a name for it and everything. They want to use it on the boy."

"And so, they can experiment on him and not let my mom use it. Her life is not worth it?"

"I want to help both your mom and his son."

"How? They are taking all of the work you did!"

"But they don't have it yet," Palila said with a smirk in her voice. "I have all of the pieces. I just need to put them together. And because they'll know I have it soon, I need you to come and get it."

That was where he was right now. The light turned green, and Bryce turned onto Palila's street. He had been over to her house so many times before that he knew it like the back of his hand. Her car wasn't there though. At least, that's what it seemed like at first. He waited for a moment in the driveway with his lights off. It was late, and he didn't want to take a chance in waking the children in the house or Mrs. Pau. When she didn't answer his text or his call, Bryce decided to get out and walk around the backside of the house to the trailer where Palila lived. That's when he saw the car. *Strange,* he thought, *she never parks in the back.* Palila was neat and clean in every way. Her clothes were color coordinated. Her car was spotless on the inside. It wasn't like she had to try hard. It was in her nature to have things neat and proper, but she wasn't OCD or anal about it. She would never park on the grass though much less drive on it. Bryce knocked on the door and realized that it was open when the door moved.

"Hey, Pae," he called out softly. "It's Bryce." There was no answer. Her trailer was just like she always left it. Immaculate. Bryce stepped inside and started to look around. The light was on in her room.

"Palila, are you in here?" Still no answer. Car there. Lights on. Bryce moved quickly to the back and into the room where his feet stopped abruptly. She was laying on the bed with her feet hanging off the bed. Her eyes were open. Her body was completely limp. Her throat had a deep laceration from where she had been strangled to death. Bryce stood in the doorway and stared for a moment. His body was confused. His mind was a mess of jumbled thoughts. She was dead. Her fear of something dangerous was legitimized at this moment.

"I wanted to hold her," he told Raine as tears came to his eyes. "She was my friend, and—she cared about people so much."

Raine stood outside not far from the house. She swallowed as he talked. "I'm sorry that you witnessed that, Bryce."

"I was so angry. The whole room was a mess, and I thought, maybe—maybe there was something still around that would help me know her killer or what happened. I don't know how it was missed by whoever killed her, but I saw that her left hand was clenched into a fist, and a little piece of paper stuck out between two fingers. I pried it open and found a piece of paper. A bank deposit slip that had writing on it that just said 'R33PM.'"

"And you knew that he was the one that was behind this?" Raine said. She closed her eyes. "And you looked at that statement, and something in your mind clicked. You knew that in order to get that serum, something serious had to happen. Something had to happen to get Painter and Edison to release that serum to you."

"Sounds like you know it all," Bryce said. "And the serum?"

"Bryce, I need you to do me a favor before I tell you."

Micah stood up slowly when Number two walked up to him and handed him the phone. He watched the gunman calmly as he put the receiver to his ear.

"Hello?"

"Oh my god, Micah." Micah felt his heart start to pound when he heard Raine's voice. "Tell me you're okay. You aren't hurt."

"I'm—I'm fine. I'm okay. What—where are you?"

"There is so much we need to talk about, and I'm—It can wait. Micah," she said with sadness in her voice, "these men are in a tough situation. I know what they've done, but it's bigger than that. They're trying to save their mother's life."

Micah listened to the quick description that Raine gave, and everything was clear. Bryce looked on with a nervous stare as did the others in the bank. Micah put down the phone after a minute and cleared his throat.

"Ted," he said to the banker. Ted stood up quickly. "There is a bank deposit box for Palila Dahni that you're going to help them get access, too."

"All of our customer deposit boxes are password protected," Ted said. "It requires a password to be keyed into the lock."

Micah looked at Bryce. "It's R33PM. Palila put the serum for you in there. She didn't think it was safe for her to have it on her, and so she came here and deposited it in her deposit box. When she left the bank and got into her car, she had written the password on the deposit slip because she was going to meet and give it to you, but she didn't get the chance."

Bryce shook his head. "So, it was here the whole time. None of this had to happen."

"No." Micah nodded to Ted who grudgingly took number one and four back to the deposit boxes. Micah caught Bryce's eyes. "I need to you to listen to me. The police are out there, and you're not going to escape them—at least not all of you."

Bryce frowned but followed Micah's gaze to his sister who was standing close by. Realization hit her and him at the same time. Macy shook her head violently. Without any regard, she peeled her mask off. "No! No!" she said. "I'm not letting you do this?"

"He's right, sis," Bryce said. "They don't know how many were involved, but they definitely don't know a girl was."

"But they do," Macy pointed to the hostages. Micah looked at everyone. All of their eyes transfixed on the scene that was going on in front of them. Bryce wasn't sure what to say to that.

"There were only three men." Micah looked at the owner of the voice. It was the mother of the little girl. She stood up slowly and pulled her daughter up with her. She nodded to Micah. "There were only three men."

Some of the others in the bank stood up and echoed the same phrase. Micah gave a sigh of relief. He turned back to Bryce.

"I will make sure that she gets out okay, and that she gets the serum to home to your mother. You have my word."

Bryce nodded slowly, and Macy grabbed him in a hug.

Micah felt a presence next to him. *Shit!* Eli's smug look hit every nerve in his body. He had forgotten about Eli. He had forgotten about the one person who truly deserved to be taken in today.

"So, you have to choose," Eli said. "You take me in, and you risk her being caught," he said nodding to Macy. "You get her out, and I promise you, I'll get away."

The hostages would be immediately checked over and questioned. The girl would be found out without a problem. He wouldn't be able to shield her from it. Eli could walk out and disappear without a problem. This was the choice. What was more important?

The others returned with the box and the serum. It was handed to the girl after it was explained what was going to happen. Father and brothers embraced their sister one last time, and then walked to the front of the bank, and set down their guns at the door before walking out—hands in the air.

Raine put down the phone. For some reason, she couldn't help it, but she started to cry. She couldn't remember the last time did cried—like really cried. It had been years. Tai walked up to her. He stood next to her for a few seconds before she laid her head on his chest and he wrapped his big beefy arms around her and just listened.

"I feel like a child," Raine said. "Why am I crying?"

"Cu Mon. You reely want me ta say it?" Tai asked. Raine sniffled and wiped some tears away.

"What? Say what?"

Tai chuckled causing his belly and chest to shake like a small earthquake. "You love him."

She let the tears settle, and for a moment, thought about how many ways she wanted to protest this statement. But she couldn't. It was at that moment that she realized the last time she cried was when she lost Donnie.

"You're right. I think that I do—love him." Tai pulled her away and looked her in the eye.

"Loa'a iā'oe ke aloha i ka wā e Ailani ai'oe."

Raine shook her head. "What does that mean?"

"It means," Tai said, " dat love wi fin you wen you need it da most. And you—ma fraand, need it."

Raine smiled. Punching him on the shoulder, she placed a hand on his shoulder. "You should probably go back to the bank. I'm sure Ailani has his hands full."

"Where you goin?" Tai frowned.

"I—I need to take an Uber somewhere. I'll call you though. I'm going to need your help with something soon." Tai frowned. "Don't worry. It'll all be clear in time."

CHAPTER SIX

Eli's head jerked up. His eyes grew wide as he looked around to get his surroundings, but-but… It was dark. His racked his brain to figure out what had happened. He remembered being in the bank when those idiots had surrendered themselves to the police when they walked out of the doors of the bank. Police had rushed them and secured them while several rushed inside and ushered out the hostages including him. He wasn't sure what Micah Duscane was going to do about getting the girl out of the bank without being noticed, but he had gone out of the back with her. He hadn't stayed around long. In the confusion of reporters, police, EMTs, and the crowd gathered around the barriers put up; he had walked out of the area. Forget the car; no one would trace it back to him.

It was registered under a fake name and fake address. No one in the bank knew who he was and probably didn't recognize him. He wasn't the center of attention most of the time. It was Micah.

He had walked far enough away, caught an Uber, and gotten dropped off at home. He had gotten inside of the front doorway before---it all went blank.

His wrists were tied. His feet were, too. Eli sat in a chair similar to the one that he had left in his basement. Actually, as his eyes adjusted, he found that he was staring at the same set up of his basement. The exact same layout. The—exact same basement.

A light came on, and his suspicions were confirmed. It was the exact same basement. He was trapped in his basement. He struggled at the ropes that were constricting his limbs.

A cough to his left caught his attention. She was in a chair just like him—constricted and bound. He couldn't see her face right away, but she had dark hair and fair skin.

"Hey!" he yelled. "Hey!"

What happened to Heather? What happened to him? He shook in the chair and tried to slam the chair down on the floor to break it. Nothing. Well, almost nothing. The girl next to him began to stir. First, it was a groan, and then some slight movement.

"Hey, wake up!"

The girl jerked awake and looked around the room just like he had when he was trying to get his bearings straight.

When she turned to him, she gasped. Of course, he did, too as her facial features became more recognizable. It had been so long since he had seen her. Her innocent and gentle eyes looked at him.

"H—Hanna?" He croaked out. Tears started to well in her eyes when Eli spoke.

"Eli? Eli, is that you?" When he nodded, she started to weep. "Oh my god, Eli! Eli, my brother!"

"Hanna! Why are you here? What are you doing here!"

"I brought her here." The voice was disguised. It seemed to be coming from a speaker somewhere in the basement. Eli didn't want to give whoever it was the satisfaction of seeing him sweat. He hated being in the vulnerable position. The voice didn't seem to care. "I brought her here to play a game."

"Let her go. If you don't, you'll have to do with me!"

"Eli," Hanna said. "Help me."

"Hanna…."

"You're in no position to beg—although I enjoy it," the voice said. "Are you ready for the game?"

"Go to hell!" Eli belted at the top of his lungs.

"The game is called who deserves to live." Eli's fist clenched behind his back. The voice continued. "You just have to decide who deserves to live—you or your sister."

Eli sat there. He refused to answer. This was stupid. Whoever this idiot was going to pay dearly for this.

"Eli, I'm scared. What is this?"

"Hanna, I—I don't' know."

'You need to make a decision, Eli. Quickly. There is a gun that is trained on her and will fire within two minutes if you don't."

"You're bluffing!" In response, a gunshot echoed throughout the basement causing him to jump. Hanna screamed.

"I don't joke," the voice said. "The fact that you have purposely not seen her in years, or the fact that your mom cheated on your dad leaving the family devastated, or the fact that you have never felt true love. You feel worthless. You feel like—you are alone."

"Whoever you are, I'm going to kill you."

"Not the name of the game, and like I said, your time in running out. You still have to choose."

"I'm not going to…" the gun fired again. This time, he saw the shot land just feet in front of Hanna.

"Fine, I choose…"

"Wait—maybe we should switch this up first. What if we ask her?"

Eil looked over to Hanna. She shook her head. "Please don't hurt him. Please don't hurt my brother. Don't. I love him."

"He doesn't deserve your love! You fool!" A third gunshot rang, and Eli watched as Hanna and her chair toppled backwards on the floor.

"No!" Eli screamed. The scene just kept replaying before his eyes. "No! No! No!"

"If only you could save her now," The voice said as if he

could open the basement door. It was clear and crisp. The voice modulation and disguise was off. Eli's eyes widened when he recognized it. It couldn't be. There's no way. He heard the footsteps come up to his chair and started to shudder. Raine's face appeared masked by the dim lighting that night appeared in the basement. Her eyes fixated on Eli as he stared at her in disbelief.

"No," he said with something of a comical revelation. "This isn't right. I'm dreaming."

"No, you aren't," Raine said. She reached out and pinched his bare arm. Eli winced. "See, not dreaming."

She stood before him now. Looking in between him and his sister. Eli growled an incoherent phrase before letting out a stream of curse words. Raine smiled. It wasn't one full of gloating. It was one that empathized with his position.

"There is no way this is happening?"

"What?" Raine nudged his leg with her foot. "There can't be a way that I'm here, and I've lured your sister here? I think you and I both know that I can do a lot of things. A lot. Especially, when you have help."

There was more movement coming from the side of Eli. What he saw next made his jaw drop. Heather, the girl he had kidnapped, drugged, and tied up in the basement, was standing in front of him with a grin on her face.

"Remember me?" she said. Raine put an arm around the girl. Eli looked over at the fallen body of his sister, and it wasn't there. The chair was there, and the ropes. Raine coughed.

"I believe that you've met, Heather. She's a good friend of mine. We met at a spin class."

"No," Eli said softly. Raine nodded.

"See, she takes acting classes as a theatre student. She is really good at it, don't you think?"

No," Eli said more forcefully. Raine continued.

"It was easy for her to create some sort of character that would draw you out. A woman that cheated on her fiancé. Who had a faithful person waiting for her even though she was a slut—a whore—someone who didn't deserve love." Eli shook as he listened to her. "It was easy. Get her to attract enough attention to where you would make her your next victim. I planted a tracking device on her, and when you were away thinking that you had a mouse in your trap, I was able to make sure that she was free. Then we just needed to find out what your weakness was—or rather who."

"But—but..." Eli didn't know what to say. For once, he was lost. The game was no longer in his control. Raine knelt down in front of him.

"What? But she looked like Hanna?" Eli felt himself nodding in slow motion. Raine nodded along with him, and slowly produced a syringe. She stared at it for a moment.

"Do you remember when you kidnapped my fiancé and injected him with poison? Do you?" Raine watched Eli's eyes look at the syringe. Meghan continued. "I had just enough for you."

"You're lying," Eli spat. Raine shrugged.

"I guess that you'll have to take that chance; either way. You're done, Eli. I win."

Eli's anger got the best of him. He jerked just enough to topple him over. As he laid on the floor, he watched Raine, who had turned her back on him. She let Heather go up the stairs first and then followed.

"This isn't how it works," Eli said.

"It doesn't," Raine said turning briefly just to have one last look at him. Their eyes met, and for a moment, Raine remembered what she went through because of him—wrong—because of her. Sure, he was twisted and demented, but she had accepted his depiction of her. That was going to change.

"Don't you leave me here!" Eli growled.

Heather walked up the stairs, and Raine followed. "Goodbye, Eli."

She ignored his screams and yelled and opened the door to the basement and came face to face with the dozens of police officers that she had called to the scene when she was sure that Eli was truly there. Of course, Tai was there, and Ailani.

"Well, you did it," Ailani said. "You caught him."

"I wan some alone time with da foo," Tai said. "I'll teach him something dat he ain't neva gon forget."

They all respected her request to let Eli stay down there

for a bit before going down to officially arrest him. She wanted him to know what it felt like. She wanted to know that he would have some understanding of what it felt like. She wanted—what she couldn't get there. For what she really wanted, she would have to go to him.

*H*er apartment had the perfect balcony. It was the best view and her favorite place to hang out. Micah sat on one end, and she on the other as they reviewed the events.

"You got her out?" Raine asked referring to the girl, Macy, whom Micah had sacrificed landing Eli for. He nodded.

"She should be on a flight back home—with a cure—at least we hope it works." There was another pause which had already happened several times that night.

"Sorry, I didn't tell you about what I was planning with Eli," she admitted. Micah shrugged.

"Sorry, I didn't tell you that he was in the bank with me."

"I guess we're even then," she laughed. "We finally caught him."

Micah nodded. He took a sip of the coffee that she had made and smiled. "He made

me realize something, you know." Raine turned her attention to him. "He made me realize that I was too afraid to be the hero. I was too afraid to realize that you deserved my love."

Had he just said what she thought he said? Raine looked at him. "What do you mean?"

"Raine, you know what I mean?" Micah laughed. "You and I have been doing this dance where you feel like you don't deserve my love, and I don't feel like I'm good enough to be that man for you. Well—um—that stops now."

Raine stared at him. "I think that's a really good idea. How do we do that?" Micah pushed himself away from the side of the balcony over to her. He was within inches of her body, and she gulped hard as she waited. Their lips touched, and all Raine could think about that moment was that she never thought she would feel this way again. It wasn't just having someone. She needed to know that love was possible again—from someone else and from her.

Micah pulled away from the kiss. "Was that okay? Or was it…."

He didn't have time to say anything. Raine brought him back in for more. She had found love, and this time, she wasn't going to let go.

ABOUT THE AUTHOR

Dylan Keefer is a web designer / developer by day and a writer by night. He's basically a modern day superhero, using code and words to breathe creativity into reality. On a more serious note, he has been writing from a very young age and has always been pursuing the dream of writing professionally. Everything he does is in pursuit of that dream. He writes light-hearted as well as dark themed stories across multiple genres. His stories involve psychological struggles or moral dilemmas of the human condition. If you like those themes and the idea of questioning what it means to be human, then it won't matter what genre the story is; he will make you a believer.

Want Free Books?

Join my newsletter to receive updates on my new book releases go to my website at purplepress.org to sign up.

Join My Newsletter

Reviews are essential to my growth. If you enjoyed this book, I would love it if you took a moment to leave a honest review on Amazon or Goodreads or both. A few sentences is plenty, just enough to let fellow readers know what you liked about this book.

Thank you in advance, we appreciate and couldn't do this without you.

For more information:
purplepress.org
PurplePressLLC@gmail.com

Demon's Match

Satan's Torment

Devil's Advocate

Lucifer's Wake

Mischief Miles Investigations

A Familiar Scent

Breaking and Entering

Like Father, Like Son

Too Close For Comfort

Mr. Right or Mr. Wrong

Everscape Online

Traitor of Golden Blaze

Queen of Ragnarok

Champion of Everscape

Britney Allen: The London Crime Syndicate

Blood of Babes: The Slasher Files

Standalone

Lost in Space

The Lone Survivor

Mr. Buddy Bot

Evelyn